MY BIG SHOUTING DAY!

To Anna Christophersen
Best wishes,
Rebecca

MY BIG SHOUTING DAY!
A JONATHAN CAPE BOOK 978 1 780 08006 2

Published in Great Britain by Jonathan Cape,
an imprint of Random House Children's Publishers UK
A Random House Group Company

This edition published 2012

5 7 9 10 8 6 4

RANDOM HOUSE CHILDREN'S PUBLISHERS UK,
61–63 Uxbridge Road, London W5 5SA

www.**randomhousechildrens**.co.uk
www.**randomhouse**.co.uk

Addresses for companies within The Random House Group Limited can be found at:
www.**randomhouse**.co.uk/offices.htm

THE RANDOM HOUSE GROUP Limited Reg. No. 954009

A CIP catalogue record for this book is available from the British Library.

Printed in China

The Random House Group Limited supports The Forest Stewardship Council® (FSC®), the leading
international forest-certification organisation. Our books carrying the FSC label are printed on FSC®-certified paper.
FSC is the only forest-certification scheme endorsed by the leading environmental organisations, including Greenpeace.
Our paper procurement policy can be found at www.randomhouse.co.uk/environment

MIX
Paper from
responsible sources
FSC® C104723

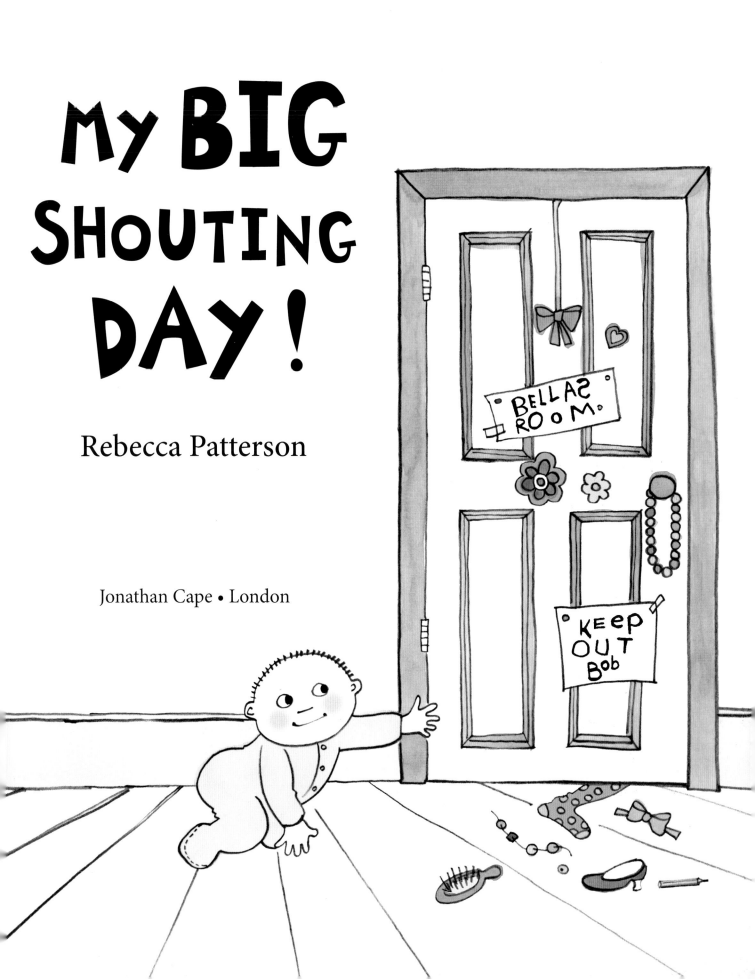

My BIG SHOUTING DAY!

Rebecca Patterson

Jonathan Cape • London

Yesterday I woke up and Bob was crawling around
  MY ROOM licking MY JEWELLERY . . .

   So I shouted:

GET OUT
OF MY ROOM!

and that was the start of MY BIG SHOUTING DAY.

Then I came downstairs and I saw THAT EGG.
 I cried and cried and said,

I CAN'T EAT THAT!

and Mummy said, "You could eat it last week.
 Look at Bob eating his mashed banana."

After the TERRIBLE EGG I didn't like my shoes either. So I took them off all by myself shouting:

NO SHOES!

And then we had to go shopping and Mummy said,
 "Please stop wriggling, Bella."
 But I couldn't stop wriggling and in the end I shouted:

GET ME OUT

Mummy said, "You will give Bob an earache.
And you are giving *me* a headache."

And Bob poked me and said, **"ear."**

At lunchtime Sasha and her mummy came to play and to have some peanut butter and grapes and a biscuit. But . . .

MY BISCUIT BROKE!

Then I couldn't play nicely and I kept saying,

NO! YOU CAN'T BE PRINCESSES!

and in the end Sasha and her mummy went home.

In the afternoon it was my ballet lesson. I said,

BALLET IS TOOO

ITCHY!

... out I was a bit loud and Mrs Clark stopped playing the piano and Miss Louisa said, "Dear, oh dear, perhaps you should sit in the corner then."

On the way home we met the lady who lives next door
and she said that Bob was the sweetest thing she'd seen
all day, and then she said, "And how is Bella?"

I was a long way behind so I had to shout:

I HAVE A HURTING FOOT!

and Mummy said could I keep my voice down and
could I PLEASE stop lying on the pavements.

Then it was time for my tea and my bath.
But those peas were

TOO HOT!

And our bath was

TOO COLD!

And I was

TOO WET!

And it was

TOO MINTY!

After that I rolled and rolled and said,

NO BED NO NO

NO NO BED NO NO

and Mummy said, "Well, I think someone needs to go to bed."

But I rolled all over my room
and then I rolled into Bob's room
and I said,

BED IS FOR BABIES!

and then I yawned,
a little yawn.

Then I crawled into my room, and Mummy said, "Who wants a story?"

and I said,

NOBODY!

But she came into my room anyway and we cuddled up
and had my best story about fairies and cake.

YAWN...

I yawned again and I said, very quietly,

"Today was a big shouting day, Mummy, sorry."

And she kissed me goodnight and said,
"I know, we all have those days sometimes,
but perhaps you will be more
cheerful tomorrow!"

And . . .

I WAS! I WAS!
I was cheerful . . .

ALL DAY

LONG!